Elephants

JoAnn Cleland

FITZGERALD BOOKS

Bethany, Missouri

Photo Credits:
Cover © Photodisc; Title Page © Corel; Page 5 © Chris Fourie; Page 6 © Hedda Gjerpen; Pages 7, 9, 12, 13, 14, 16, 22 © Photodisc; Page 10 © Jeff Gynane; Page 17 © Cay-Uwe Kulzer; Pages 19, 21 © Corel; Page 20 © Simone Van Den Berg; Page 21 © Carrie Winegarden

Cataloging-in-Publication Data

Cleland, Joann
    Elephants / JoAnn V. Cleland. — 1st ed.
    p. cm. — (Animals in danger)

    Includes bibliographical references and index.
    Summary: Examines the physical characteristics, behavior, and habitat of elephants and why they are endangered.
    ISBN-13: 978-1-4242-1388-7 (lib. bdg. : alk. paper)
    ISBN-10: 1-4242-1388-6 (lib. bdg. : alk. paper)
    ISBN-13: 978-1-4242-1478-5 (pbk. : alk. paper)
    ISBN-10: 1-4242-1478-5 (pbk. : alk. paper)

    1. Elephants—Juvenile literature. 2. Endangered species—Juvenile literature. 3. Wildlife conservation—Juvenile literature. [1. Elephants. 2. Endangered species. 3. Rare animals. 4. Wildlife conservation.] I. Cleland, Joann. II. Title. III. Series.
    QL737.P98C54 2007
    599.67—dc22

First edition
© 2007 Fitzgerald Books
802 N. 41st Street, P.O. Box 505
Bethany, MO 64424, U.S.A.
Printed in China
Library of Congress Control Number: 2006940870

Table of Contents

How Big Are Elephants?

When this baby elephant was born, he weighed about 200 pounds. How much do you think a grown-up elephant weighs?

An adult African elephant is very big. He can weigh as much as 16,000 pounds. That is as heavy as a big truck.

An elephant can grow to be 11 feet tall.
That is as tall as a one-story house!

What Do Elephants Eat?

Elephants use their **trunks**, **tusks**, and teeth to gather and chew food. They eat nothing but plants.

Tusk

Trunk

An adult elephant eats about 300 pounds of food every day. That is like 300 huge heads of lettuce!

Where Do Elephants Live?

You may see elephants in the zoo, but that is not their real habitat or home. Do you know where they roam free?

Savannas

Most elephants live in Africa. They roam flat grasslands called **savannas**.

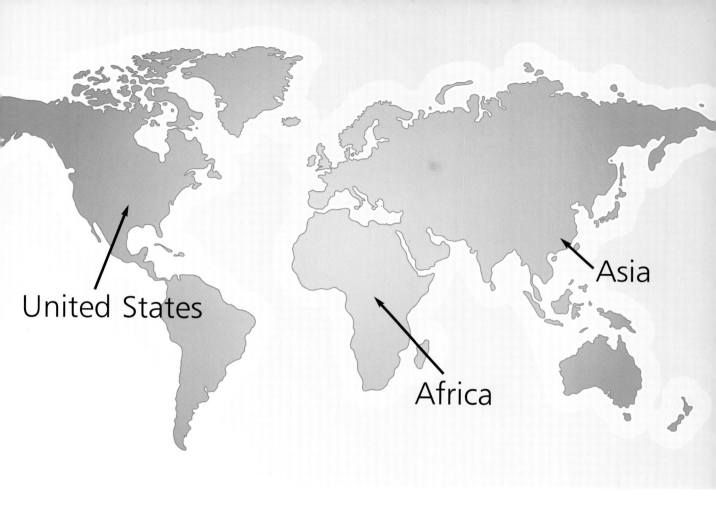

Some elephants live in Asia. Asian
elephants are smaller than African elephants.

16

Elephants are favorites of visitors going on African **safaris**.

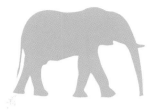

How Many Elephants Are There?

Forty years ago, there were over a million elephants living in the world.

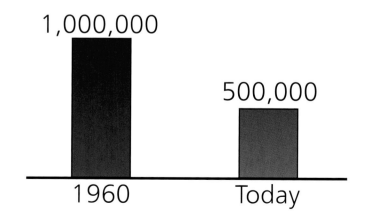

1,000,000

500,000

1960   Today

Today there are only about 500,000.
Why do you think there are so few now?

Will Elephants Become Extinct?

People kill elephants mostly for their **ivory** tusks. Ivory is very valuable.

Ivory Tusk

Valuable
Ivory Carving

21

It is against the law to shoot elephants. Elephants will not become **extinct** if everyone obeys the law.

Glossary

extinct (ek STINGKT) — gone from the Earth forever

ivory (EYE vur ee) — what tusks are made of

safari (suh FAH ree) — a guided sightseeing trip

savanna (suh VAN uh) — a large grassland

trunk (TRUHNGK) — an elephant's long nose

tusks (TUHSKS) — an elephant's long, pointed front teeth

Index

FURTHER READING

Anderson, Jill. *Elephants*. Northwood, 2006.
Eckart, Edana. *African Elephant*. Rosen Book Works, 2003.
Searl, Duncan. *Elephants*. Bearport Publishing, 2006.

WEBSITES TO VISIT

Because Internet links change so often, Fitzgerald Books has developed an online list of websites related to the subject of this book. This site is updated regularly. Please use this link to access the list: www.fitzgeraldbookslinks.com/ad/ele

ABOUT THE AUTHOR

Jo Cleland, Professor Emeritus of Reading Education, taught in public education and at the College of Education at Arizona State University West. Jo continues to work with children through her storytelling and workshops. She has presented to audiences of teachers across the nation and the world, bringing to all her favorite message: What we learn with delight, we never forget.